WITHDRAWN

JUN 2 9 2021

NAFC PUBLIC LIBRARY

YP YO
Young, James, 1956- DEC 0 7 2016
  Penelope and the pirates : being the
exciting tale of a young cat and her

D1415981

Dear Parent:

Books mean many things to people. Books can represent an afternoon's reading or a special holiday gift. Books can even become prized possessions.

Children can acquire the skill of handling books with care. **Designating a bookcase or special place for books to be kept will help your child develop a sense of ownership and pride.** Handling books with clean hands, learning to turn the pages gently, putting books back where they belong—these are all habits that parents can instill in their children. And don't worry: if a book is torn, it can usually be repaired with adhesive tape.

We hope that *Penelope & the Pirates* becomes one of your child's favorite (and most read) books.

Sincerely,

Stephen Fraser

Stephen Fraser
Senior Editor
Weekly Reader Books

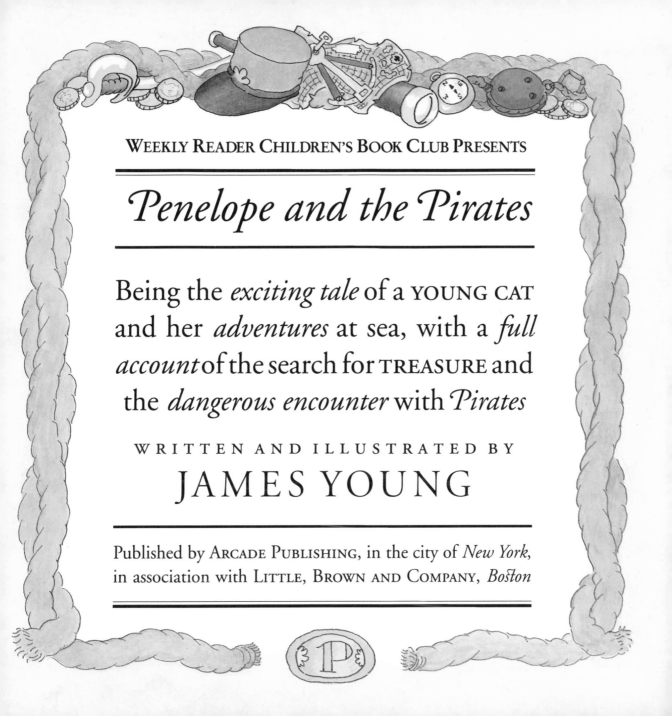

WEEKLY READER CHILDREN'S BOOK CLUB PRESENTS

Penelope and the Pirates

Being the *exciting tale* of a YOUNG CAT and her *adventures* at sea, with a *full account* of the search for TREASURE and the *dangerous encounter* with *Pirates*

WRITTEN AND ILLUSTRATED BY

JAMES YOUNG

Published by ARCADE PUBLISHING, in the city of *New York*, in association with LITTLE, BROWN AND COMPANY, *Boston*

This book is a presentation of Newfield Publications, Inc. Newfield Publications offers book clubs for children from preschool through high school. For further information write: **Newfield Publications, Inc.**, 4343 Equity Drive, Columbus, Ohio 43228.

Published by arrangement with Arcade Publishing, Inc., a Little, Brown company. Newfield Publications is a federally registered trademark of Newfield Publications, Inc. Weekly Reader is a federally registered trademark of Weekly Reader Corporation.

Copyright © 1990 James Young
All rights reserved. No part of this book may be reproduced in any form or by any electronic or mechanical means, including information storage and retrieval systems, without permission in writing from the publisher, except by a reviewer who may quote brief passages in a review.

First Edition Library of Congress Catalog Card Number 90-81076
Library of Congress Cataloging-in-Publication information is available.
ISBN: 1-55970-074-2

Published in the United States by Arcade Publishing, Inc., New York, a Little, Brown company
Published simultaneously in Canada by Little, Brown, & Company (Canada) Limited

Designed by Marc Cheshire

1 3 5 7 9 10 8 6 4 2

Penelope was a wharf cat. She had three black spots and a long black tail of which she was very proud. Other than that her life was not very exciting.

One day she decided to do something about it. She packed her bag and set off down the wharf.

"I'm Penelope," she said, stepping up smartly to an official-looking gentleman. "I'd like to sign aboard, sir."

"Ned's my name, Captain of the *Sweetwater*," replied the official-looking gentleman. "And just what do you do?"

"I catch mice," answered Penelope.

"There are no mice on my ship," said Captain Ned.

"I can be a look-out," said Penelope.

"Sorry, I already have a look-out."

Then Penelope had an idea. "Do you see this fine tail and these three black spots on my back?" she asked.

"How could I not?" replied Captain Ned.

"Well," said the cat, "this is no ordinary tail and these are not just ordinary

spots. They are a map leading to a wonderful treasure."

"Why, that's an entirely different situation," said Captain Ned. "Welcome aboard!"

They did not realize the entire conversation had been overheard by a pirate.

The next day the *Sweetwater* set sail. She was not alone.

For many days they sailed the seas and each day was better than the one before. Penelope played on the poop deck and clambered in the rigging. She even did look-out duty in the crow's nest, although she didn't see any crows.

But most of the time she spent curled up in Captain Ned's lap fast asleep.
They became very fond of each other.

One night, while everyone was sleeping, pirates took the ship!

They tied Captain Ned and his crew to the mizzenmast. But they took Penelope with them because, of course, she had the map.

For many days they sailed through rough and stormy seas, and every day Penelope missed Captain Ned more and more. She worried about what would happen when the pirates discovered that her long black tail and the black spots on her back were just a tail and spots.

Then one day the look-out cried "LAND HO!"
And there was land—three small islands just like the spots on Penelope's back and one long island just like her long black tail.

The pirates went ashore and started digging. Still Penelope worried.

Suddenly, the pirates cried "YO HO!" They had found a chest filled with jewels and golden doubloons.

No one was more surprised than Penelope.

Now that the pirates had the treasure they no longer needed Penelope. They decided to make her walk the plank.

Just then there was a blast of trumpets! It was Captain Ned!

He kept the pirates busy with his fancy swordwork while Penelope dazzled them with her long black tail.

At last the ship was theirs, as was the treasure. But more important, Penelope and Captain Ned were together again.

"How did you find me?" Penelope asked. "After all, I was the only map."

"That's easy," said Captain Ned. "You spent so much time in my lap, I memorized you."

So, with the treasure safely stowed and the *Sweetwater's*
bow turned toward home, Penelope curled up
in Captain Ned's lap once more
and they both took
a long nap.